ARTHUR'S AMULET

Jan Davie

ATHENA PRESS
LONDON

ISBN 1 84401 228 X

First Published 2004 by
ATHENA PRESS
Queen's House, 2 Holly Road
Twickenham TW1 4EG
United Kingdom

Printed and bound by Antony Rowe Ltd, Eastbourne

ARTHUR'S AMULET

For John and Paul,
who have always believed in me.

Chapter One

I T WAS MONDAY. SCHOOL, BUT NOT AN ORDINARY school day. Assembly was cancelled, and Year Six were in the hall, a chattering and excited bunch, dressed in jeans and cagoules, shouldering fat rucksacks and heaving stuffed suitcases into the corner by the door. Tom came in last, on his own, and scowled at the gathering of children, parents and teachers. 'Coach is here,' he stated.

The announcement initiated a flurry of goodbyes and embarrassing kisses, teachers waving lists and placating last minute anxieties voiced by parents who, in many cases, had not let their little darlings out of their sight for a minute before, and certainly not for as long as a whole week! The head teacher appeared and gave the customary lecture on good behaviour and then it was time to go.

Mr Gladwell organised the children into twos and led them out to the coach. 'Fred Braithwaite and Charlie Cooper, Tom Harper and Joe Smith...' he read from his list. '...Jay Parker and Eddie Price, Pip Wilkes and Nicky Ramshaw...' They swarmed onto the bus as their names were read out. '...Chris Brown and Lesley Harris, Trish Dunfly and Lol Kemp, Andy Brennen and Sam

Robarts. Sit down and fasten your seat belts. Yes, Tom Harper, fasten it. We've paid extra for this expression of concern for your well-being, so use it!'

The list continued and the bus filled as Miss Priestly and Mrs Duffy, and a handful of willing parents, loaded the bags into the boot. The two teachers climbed on board with the driver – a portly, red-faced, middle-aged man who had already made his feelings on 'blasted kids' very clear – and counted heads.

'Thirty,' declared Miss Priestly.

'Thirty,' agreed Mrs Duffy, nodding to the driver, and the coach crunched out of the car park as the cluster of parents waved.

'I think I've forgotten...' Lol began. The children and teachers moaned and the driver turned around, peering petulantly down the aisle.

'It will have to stay forgotten, Lol Kemp,' said Mr Gladwell firmly.

The driver looked relieved and turned his attention back to the road, heaving a long sigh.

'Now settle down everyone!' said Miss Priestly. 'We've a long journey ahead and I want a peaceful, stress-free one. Understood?'

'Some hope of that,' whispered Pip to Nicky. 'I can't believe they've let Tom Harper come with us.'

'He'll be okay with Joe here.'

'I just hope he's not in our group,' Pip said.

Sam turned around and leaned through the gap

in the seats. 'Who don't you want in your group, Pip?' he asked, loudly enough for the whole coach to hear.

Pip squirmed. 'Shut up, Sam,' she hissed.

'Tom Harper, isn't it?'

'Sam Robarts, sit down at once!' Mr Gladwell commanded, and Sam's head disappeared in a flash. Tom glared out of the window and clenched his fists.

'Take no notice,' said Joe, soothingly. Tom did not reply.

Chapter Two

THE JOURNEY WAS AMAZINGLY CALM AND FREE OF stress; a couple of false alarms for the sick bag, but that was about all. Even the service station stops had passed without incident, although the sullen look on the driver's face conveyed the message to the public-at-large that transporting these 'blasted kids' was the most burdensome job in the world.

After the second stop Pip fell asleep as the drone of teachers' voices and the swish of the tyres on the motorway lulled her. She awoke with a start as the coach swung heavily around an impossibly tight bend, lurching the passengers from left to right.

'I hope we don't meet anything coming in the opposite direction,' muttered Mrs Duffy darkly.

The driver stiffened slightly but did not drop his speed. Pip looked out of the window. They were off the motorway and in the countryside, weaving along a narrow, winding road.

'It's like being in a maze with all those high hedges on either side of us,' Nicky said. 'It's like being in a different world.'

'We'll be back on the main road soon,' said Mr Gladwell. 'Nearly there,' said Miss Priestly cheerfully.

The coach turned onto a large duel carriageway and then, almost immediately, turned sharply left and entered a dark, tree-lined, single-track lane. There was a sign, partly obscured by branches, but they could all read 'Ashfields' written on it. 'Yes!' shouted Sam.

The trees grew more dense, and they could see forested hills climbing away into the sky. As the driver negotiated the tight corners, they caught glimpses of a tall, stone house buried high in the greenery. Suddenly it was in front of them, and the coach juddered to a halt on the curved, pebbled driveway.

'At flippin' last!' growled Tom, giving a parting scowl to the driver.

'Blasted kids,' he retorted, and heaved himself out of his seat to get the luggage from the boot.

The children tumbled stiffly onto the ground behind Tom, and stretched their legs, glad to be off.

Aided by the teachers, the driver lugged their bags onto the drive, then climbed back on board and left in a swirl of pebbles, a happy man.

Chapter Three

O VER HERE,' CALLED MR GLADWELL, AND THEY crowded around him, waiting to find out what to do next.

'First of all we are going into the annex where you will be assigned to your groups, then you will be told which rooms you are in, and then you will go there and wait for us to bring up your bags so you can unpack. Any questions?' Mr Gladwell looked around with the air of a man who was not prepared to answer, even if there had been any.

The front door of the house opened and a small, weather-beaten man, dressed in the uniform of a serious outdoor type, appeared. He strode towards Mr Gladwell, his right hand outstretched.

'Phil,' he said, 'great to see you again.'

The two men shook hands and exchanged hearty greetings.

'This is Peter,' Mr Gladwell explained, 'our leader for the week.'

Peter turned and smiled at everyone, his bright blue eyes glancing at the children, summing them up.

'Follow me,' he said abruptly and walked off. The children followed meekly behind, totally overwhelmed by the strangeness of the huge

Victorian house. Peter took them past the large front door and the rows of church-like, pointed windows, to a new addition to the building, long and low like a Swiss chalet. They went in. It smelled of pine and mud.

They were in a large meeting room, sparsely furnished, except for a semi-circle of plastic chairs. The children sat down feeling awkward and nervous. Two other adults arrived, dressed like Peter, and were introduced; Clare and Steve, also outdoor pursuit leaders, who would be taking charge of groups two and three, respectively. There were two others still to come who would be taking the fourth group.

Their teachers arrived, Mr Gladwell clutching his lists, Mrs Duffy looking anxiously around the group, checking to see that they were all there, and finally, Miss Priestly, who hurried over to the leaders and started talking quietly and earnestly with them.

'Right, listen up,' said Mr Gladwell. 'These are your groups. When you know which one you are in, I want you to follow the leaders assigned to you and go into your meeting room.' A hush descended as the children listened. 'Group One is with Peter and Miss Priestly. They are: Sam Robarts, Fred Braithwaite, Jay Parker, Nicky Ramshaw, Lol Kemp, Andy Brennan, Tom Harper, Pip Wilkes, Chris Brown and Trish Dunfly...'

Pip shot a look of pure panic at Nicky, but she just shrugged her shoulders as they stood up to

11

follow Peter into a little room leading off the main one.

'...Group Two is with Mrs Duffy and Steve,' continued Mr Gladwell. Peter ushered Group One into the room and shut the door.

They were in a small, tunnel-like room, furnished with low benches on either side and rows of pegs and racks above them. They sat, and Peter beamed at them as he sat down too. 'This is our group room where we will meet each day and plan our activities. This is our headquarters, and we need a name for it to put on the door, so you can give some thought to that. In a moment, Miss Priestly will tell you which rooms you are in, and then you can go and unpack.' He stood up briskly. 'Meet you back here in half an hour to issue you with equipment and gear, then we'll have a walk around the grounds and by then it will be time for your evening meal.'

'Yes!' exclaimed Fred. 'Food at last!'

Peter opened the door and left.

Before anyone could say anything, the door opened and Miss Priestly walked in. 'Right,' she said. 'There are some rooms with four bunks and others with six, so the girls will be in...' she scanned the list she was holding carefully. '...Yes, the girls will be in Room Two, and the boys in Room Seven. Follow me.'

She led them into the big room, then out into a long, pine corridor lined with doors. 'These are the showers and toilets,' she informed them as she opened a battered door, which had once been the back door of the main house, and ushered them up a long, winding staircase. 'Here you are. Room Two.' She opened a huge panelled door onto a dim room. 'Ah, good. Your bags are already here. See you later. Come on boys.'

The girls stood in the doorway as Miss Priestly and the lads walked down the corridor, turned left and disappeared.

'I bagsy top bunk!' yelled Lol, and she hurtled into the room, breaking the silence and galvanising the girls into action.

Chapter Four

THE ROOM WAS SQUARE WITH A HIGH CEILING AND a huge bay window overlooking the drive. The furniture was dark and battered and it smelled of polish and plastic. The plastic smell emitted from the bright blue mattresses on the bunks. Lol bounced about on hers. 'Not bad,' she announced. 'Where do we put our stuff?'

'In here,' Nicky said as she opened the door of a tall, coffin-like wardrobe, located at the end of the beds.

'Where's my bag?' asked Lol. 'Oh no! They've forgotten mine.'

'Well, go and get it,' said Trish. 'Oh, all right, I'll come with you…'

They left the room and Pip and Nicky started to unpack. 'Why our group?' sighed Pip.

'He had to be in one, and I've told you, he'll be all right with Joe around,' replied Nicky.

'But Joe isn't in the group, is he?' whined Pip.

'Pip, it'll be all right,' said Nicky.

Just then Lol and Trish burst into the room with Lol's bag and a handful of school exercise books.

'What are those for?' Nicky enquired.

'To keep our daily diary in,' Lol scowled. 'Teachers!'

They unpacked quickly and were just about to leave to go to their meeting when Trish whispered, 'Shh! What's that?'

They all listened intently. They could hear voices, apparently coming from the bunks Pip and Nicky had chosen... Lol dived onto the mattress of the bottom bed. 'There's a door here!' she exclaimed and she squeezed herself between it and the bed and started pushing the bunks into the room.

'Stop it,' hissed Pip nervously. 'You shouldn't do that.'

The bunk scraped across the floorboards noisily, leaving deep grooves in the polish.

'There,' she announced proudly. 'A door.'

Sure enough, there was a door, exactly like the one leading into the corridor. Lol tried the handle and pushed. 'It won't open,' she said.

'Try pulling,' suggested Trish.

She did, and the door opened so suddenly that she fell back onto the other girls. They ended up sprawled on the floor.

'What the...?' said a voice, and the girls rolled over to see the male contingency of Group One staring down at them in amazement.

Chapter Five

THERE WAS NO TIME TO DISCUSS THE ADJOINING door, as Group One had to leave to go to the meeting. There was something about Peter that made them instinctively know that you didn't keep him waiting.

When they got to the room, they found it full of boots, helmets, waterproofs and all the paraphernalia necessary for outdoor activities. They were assigned their numbered gear and told, in no uncertain terms, by Peter that the equipment, its condition and return, was their responsibility. They hung their stuff on the pegs and lined up their boots and helmets on the racks. They were then led to the Drying room. This was a long, oblong room on the opposite side of the corridor to the showers lined with wooden racks from floor to ceiling, where they would leave their gear after the activities. A few forlorn, forgotten socks lay over the racks. The smell was quite awful; a mixture of mud, sweat, plastic and mould. Pip gazed around the room. She was beginning to wish she had never opted to come. No one had mentioned anything about needing a drying room, especially not when Peter had shown sun-drenched slides to the parents and children all those weeks ago in the school hall... She sighed heavily.

'What's matter with you then, scared of getting wet?' sneered Tom.

'Leave me alone,' muttered Pip.

They were led back to the meeting room where they sat on the semicircle of chairs as the other groups drifted in. The teachers and leaders took their seats. Peter asked if there were any questions. This enquiry led to a flurry of hands going up and a barrage of worries, concerns and enquiries from most of the children. These were met with calm, sympathetic answers from Peter, Clare and Steve.

Pip sat silent in abject misery. It all sounded awful. She dreaded canoeing, and the thought of abseiling filled her with nothing short of terror. All this and the hateful Tom Harper in her group to mock and laugh and tease... Pip suddenly realised that the talking had stopped and saw Peter rise to his feet.

'You have time now to go to your rooms and settle in, then we'll take you on the promised tour of the grounds before dinner. We'll see you at the front entrance in an hour, and wrap up warm; the weather's looking pretty grim.'

With that, he and the other two leaders left the room. The teachers looked at the anxious faces around them.

'You'll be fine,' Mrs Duffy assured them. 'I understand the food here's great!'

'Oh yeah!' exclaimed Fred. 'I'm starving! Do we have to go on this stupid walk first?'

'The walk, far from being stupid,' sighed Mr Gladwell, 'will familiarise you with your surroundings. I trust you will be ready at the appointed time?'

'Yes, Mr Gladwell,' they intoned, drearily.

'Come on then,' said Miss Priestly. 'Up to your rooms.'

Chapter Six

WHEN THEY GOT BACK TO THEIR ROOM IT WAS exactly as they had left it. The bunk was nearly halfway across the room and the adjoining door was open. The girls waited until the boys were back. 'Hi,' said Lol through the open door.

'Get that shut and move the bunk back,' growled Tom. 'I don't want to see any more of you than I absolutely have to.'

'Fine with me!' said Pip, and she started to move the beds.

'Hang on,' said Lol. 'It could be cool; midnight feasts and everything…'

'Count me in,' said Fred.

'But we can't leave the room like this,' Trish cut in. 'I think someone might notice.'

'Put the bunk back, but a bit further away from the wall. We'll be able to open the door just enough to get in and out,' suggested Andy.

'Just get it over with,' grumbled Tom.

So the girls did as Andy suggested and, apart from the scratch marks on the floor, the room looked okay.

'I don't want them to be able to get in,' said Pip.

'Don't be silly, this could be really great,' said Trish, lying on her bunk. 'Really, really great…'

Miss Priestly appeared at the door. 'There will

be a room inspection every morning, so you must keep your area neat and tidy. Now get out your diaries, put today's date and begin your reports.'

'I've forgotten to bring a pen,' said Lol.

Miss Priestly produced a fistful of pens and pencils from her bag. 'Choose,' she smiled, and left.

'It's not fair,' muttered Lol. 'What can we write? Nothing's happened yet.' She eyed the dividing door. 'Nothing we want them to know about, I mean…'

Outside, darkness was falling. Pip went over to the window and looked out. The house was surrounded by steep, wooded hills, and there appeared to be a lake or river in front of the building, down a steep, overgrown lawn. She shuddered. It was spooky in the gathering gloom, and she wanted to be at home. A single tear rolled down her cheek.

'Come on, Pip. It's nearly time to go.'

Nicky was standing beside her. At least Nicky was with her. Things weren't quite so bad. As she struggled into her cagoule it started to rain heavily.

It carried on raining while Peter and the teachers showed them around the grounds. It was an enormous place, and the dark woods around them seemed to join the sky. It was so quiet. There was no swish and hum of traffic – there wasn't any – and the sky above was black; no glow from street lights – there weren't any of those either. It was like being in a different world. Lastly, they were shown the lake where they might canoe if the weather was too bad to go elsewhere.

Pip felt a sense of impending doom, and it did not leave her, even after they had returned to the house and eaten a warming meal. The others chatted excitedly around her while the teachers and leaders talked of climbing, abseiling, gorge-walking, canoeing and other tortures to come. She sat wrapped in dread.

Bedtime arrived and the children got ready. Pyjamas, sponge bags and cuddly toys were located; teeth cleaned, hair brushed, faces washed. They climbed into the unfamiliar bunk beds and settled down. The teachers sat on the stairs after lights out, waiting for the chatter to die down. Mrs Duffy was worried about Pip – she'd looked so forlorn all evening. But Mr Gladwell assured her that outdoor pursuits would be the making of her. 'Make her into what?' asked Mrs Duffy.

'You know what I mean,' he replied, and he turned off the landing light and they went down to the teachers' lounge.

Chapter Seven

A S SOON AS THE TEACHERS LEFT, THERE WAS A quiet knock on the adjoining door.

'Come in,' whispered Trish.

The boys pushed through the gap one by one; Sam, Fred, Jay, Andy and Chris, all with lit torches.

'Where's Tom?' asked Nicky.

'He didn't want to come,' said Chris. 'You know what he's like…'

'Hey, it's great in here, you've got lots more space,' said Sam. 'And this massive window, wow! What's out there?'

'The front. You can see the lake and everything,' said Lol.

'Cool,' declared Sam.

'Anyone got any food?' asked Fred.

'I've got some crisps left from my packed lunch,' Nicky said. 'They're a bit squashed though.'

Fred grabbed the flat packet, shook it vigorously, sat down next to her on the bunk and started munching. 'What you got there?'

Lol leaned down from her bunk, 'You know her. It's a book, all about where we are – boring.'

'It is not boring,' replied Nicky, and she continued reading, the pages illuminated by the light of her torch.

Pip joined Sam at the window and was looking out into the darkness wondering if it would ever stop raining when she spotted two red lights, very close together, moving about below, near where she knew the lake was. She gave a little yelp of surprise.

'What's up?' asked Sam.

'Those red lights down there. Can you see them?'

'Where? Oh yeah, they're moving, they're coming towards the house!' The others joined them at the window.

'There's nothing there,' said Andy, and he closed the curtains.

Nicky's eyes lit up. An opportunity like this was not to be missed by a natural storyteller like her. 'I know what they are,' she said mysteriously.

'What?' asked Chris.

'Well, around here there are stories, stories of ghosts and goblins, spectres and spooks, and the Gwyllgi. They are the Dogs of Darkness, whose red eyes glow in the night.'

There were a few gasps.

'Rubbish!' said Andy. 'There're no such things.'

'It's true. You know the Sherlock Holmes story, *The Hound of the Baskervilles*?'

They all nodded eagerly.

'Well, that's based on the Clwyd Dogs of Darkness.' She looked around her audience; they were hooked, even Andy, so she continued; 'Lots of people have seen them, they're the size of young bulls and they have shaggy black coats and flaming red eyes that burn in the dark. They pounce on lonely travellers—'

'Why?' interrupted Pip nervously.

'To eat them!'

'Gross!' said Jay. 'Go on.'

'But worse, far worse than the Gwyllgi are the Cwn Annwn, the Hounds of the Underworld. They have sleek grey and red spotted fur and burning eyes. Their baying freezes the blood of anyone who hears them. They stalk their victims and sniff out their souls, and if they have committed any sin they pounce and kill and carry off the soul to hell—'

'What's going on?'

Tom had entered through the adjoining door and he stood, surveying the torchlit scene in the room; Nicky standing with her fists clenched in a dramatic pose, and the rest of them gazing up at her with pale faces and wide eyes.

'Nicky's been telling stupid ghost stories,' said Andy. But his voice didn't come out quite as he had intended.

'They can't be that stupid, you all look scared to death.'

'It is weird here though,' said Sam, getting to his feet. It's like we're in another world. You said so yourself, Nicky, on the bus, remember?'

'Where are we, anyway?' asked Trish suddenly. Geography had never been her strong point. They could be on the Planet Zog, for all she knew.

'Hang on,' said Chris, and he stood up and went

into the next room. He returned in seconds with a map which he spread out carefully on the floor.

'Swot!' snarled Tom, and he went over to the window, snatched back the curtain and glared out into the night.

'Here,' Chris pointed to a place name circled in red pen. 'But I can't pronounce it.'

Nicky leaned over his shoulder. 'Llangynhafal,' she said.

'Very impressive,' said Tom sarcastically.

'My dad's Welsh, and I picked up the lingo a bit, from him,' she explained and put her tongue out at Tom's back.

'We're in Moel Famau Country Park, in Clwyd,' said Chris.

'The Clwyd Dogs of Darkness,' whispered Pip, her face a mask of fear.

Tom turned quickly from the window. 'You lot make me sick! I'm going to bed and leaving you silly little babies to your stupid stories.' And he stormed out of the room. 'I wish Joe was in the group,' he said as a parting shot, 'then I'd have somebody sensible to talk to.' They heard the bunk creak as he flopped angrily into bed.

'So do I,' said Jay. 'He's the only one who can stand Tom.'

'He's horrible,' declared Pip.

'I heard that,' came Tom's voice. 'I'm warning you, you little scaredy-cat, I can be much more horrible than this! We're canoeing tomorrow remember, so watch out!'

Pip gave a little sob.

'Don't listen to him,' said Sam. 'It'll be cool tomorrow, dead cool.'

The boys drifted away, and the connecting door shut with a click. The girls got back into bed murmuring sleepy 'goodnights' and drifted off to sleep.

Pip lay in the darkness listening to the sounds of other people sleeping, wishing she could join them, but whenever she closed her eyes she could see the two red dots, close together, just like eyes, moving steadily closer and closer to the house. Eventually she did sleep, but her slumber was full of dreadful dreams.

Chapter Eight

THE NEXT MORNING THEY WERE AWOKEN BY THE teachers knocking – unnecessarily loudly in the children's opinion – on the bedroom doors at half past seven!

There was a scramble for the showers and washrooms, then they went to breakfast and found all sorts of cereals to choose from and the delicious smell of bacon cooking coming from the bustling kitchen.

Peter, Clare and Steve were there, ready and eager to go. Pip could feel their enthusiasm as she walked through the door, and her heart sank.

When they had finished eating, they went into the little meeting room.

'Any ideas for a name yet?' Peter asked. There was no reply. 'Never mind, perhaps today's adventures will inspire you.' He told them all about the art of canoeing and the need for safety first – at all times, and all the fun they'd have.

It felt like a death sentence to Pip.

He jotted down the name of the place they were going to and left them to find out as much as they could about it.

'I'll get my map,' said Chris.

'Bring my books too,' Nicky called, as he dashed out of the room.

Pip sighed and picked up the lifejacket they had each been instructed to wear. 'Scared of drowning, are you?' sneered Tom.

'Leave her alone,' said Nicky.

'Why should I? She's the one who started it, calling me names.'

'She's never been canoeing before, that's all,' explained Nicky.

'Neither have I,' said Sam. 'It'll be cool.'

'Cool,' said Lol. 'Oh, you'll be cool when they make you do a roll!'

'What's a roll?' asked Sam.

Lol and Andy, who'd been canoeing before with the club they went to at home, launched into a graphic description of an eskimo roll and Pip's heart thudded so hard in her chest she thought she was going to faint! 'They won't make us do that!' she exclaimed, just as Chris dived in through the door.

'Got them.' He threw a handful of books to Nicky and unfolded his map and smoothed it out on the wooden floor. 'We're going here,' he said. '"Yes-something". Nicky, what's it say?'

'Ysgeifiog,' she said. 'Jay, you look for it in here,' and she handed him one of her books. 'Sam, you look in this one.'

There was silence for a moment as the three children scanned the books.

Pip caught Tom's eye and he glared at her, twisting his mouth into an ugly grimace. She dropped her gaze, giving Chris's map her full attention.

'Here it is!' said Jay. 'I've got it. It's an artificial lake, created in the eighteenth century to provide fishing water. Apparently there's a cave at the bottom of the lake called the Cave of the Shaggy Rocks or…'

He handed the book to Nicky, who read, '"Ogof y Graig Siagus".'

Peter appeared with Miss Priestly, fully kitted out for the day ahead.

'Something amusing you?' she enquired from beneath her vivid orange safety helmet.

'No, Miss Priestly,' they said, and burst out laughing.

Tom snarled, 'Are we going then, or what?'

'In a moment. What's your name?' asked Peter sharply.

'Tom, Tom Harper.'

'Right then, Tom Harper, what exactly have you found out about our destination today?'

'Ask them,' he muttered and looked down at the floor, his eyes blazing with embarrassment.

Jay, Nicky and Chris told Peter all they had found out. He smiled at the group, 'You've done your homework. Excellent, excellent.' He picked up Nicky's books, turning them over in his slim brown hands. 'I can see we are all going to get along splendidly, which is good, as outdoor pursuit activities bring out the best –' he paused for a moment and looked at Tom, ' – and the worst in people. We could find ourselves in a situation this week where our trust in each other is pushed to the limit, and you will need to find hidden strengths in yourselves in order to meet the challenges ahead. He stopped and looked at them each in turn, then, when he got to Tom, he suddenly beamed his one-hundred-and-fifty-watt smile directly at him. 'Let's get going!'

They piled into the minibus in the morning sunshine. Peter's enthusiasm and charm were working on them all – even Pip and Tom found themselves actually looking forward to the day ahead.

Chapter Nine

C ANOEING WAS WONDERFUL. THE WEATHER WAS beautiful and the water on the lake was still and clear. Peter and Miss Priestly were so confident in the water themselves and of the abilities of their charges that they quickly had the whole group out in single crafts, paddling for all they were worth. They had races and games. They lashed the canoes in pairs and in threes and raced again. Finally they paddled around on their own, enjoying their new-found skills. The dreaded roll was not mentioned – much to the relief of the majority of them. Everything had been perfect, except for Tom, who had suffered the indignity of being towed in by Miss Priestly from the middle of the lake, where he'd got stranded because he had dropped his paddle overboard. Peter pretended to be cross at the loss of a valuable piece of equipment, but everyone could see that he had found the incident most amusing.

They ate their packed lunches – thick sandwiches and juicy apples prepared for them by the kitchen staff at the centre – sitting on the grass by the edge of the lake. Suddenly the sky darkened and thick drops of rain began to fall.

'Quick! Everyone into the bus!' shouted Peter.

They hastily collected their things and dived for cover.

'Any grub left?' enquired Fred. Everyone groaned.

'You're quiet, Tom,' remarked Lol innocently. He turned his back on her, his cheeks burning, and pulled off his boots and drained the water out, one by one, through the open door.

Peter's head appeared over the driver's seat. 'Got your map?' he asked.

'Yes,' said Chris producing it from the depth of his cagoule beginning to open it out.

'Find where we are.'

'Got it.'

'Now find Nannerch.'

'Yes.'

'We're heading in that direction, then we'll do some exploring,' he announced. He turned around abruptly and started the engine.

'What!' exploded Tom. 'Exploring in this weather? I'm already soaked.' Miss Priestly turned and gave him a look that should have turned him to stone. He looked at the floor in sulky submission.

'I trust the arrangements for this afternoon meet with everyone else's approval,' she said firmly, and everyone nodded with enthusiasm.

Tom carried on sulking. They passed Nannerch, turned left down a single-track road and travelled cautiously along, the high, dark green hedges on both sides obscuring the view. The children talked little; Tom's dark mood, the heavy sky and the thundering rain had dampened their once high spirits.

Peter pulled off the road into a car park and stopped. 'Everybody out!' he commanded, and they filed out of the sliding door and stood in a sorry huddle as the rain poured out of the slate-grey heavens. 'Up there,' Peter informed them, utterly unmoved by the weather conditions, 'is a Moel – a hill.'

They lifted their heads dutifully and blinked towards where he was pointing. Sure enough, there was a grass-covered, conical hill rising above them.

'We'll climb to the top – any route you like – and we'll meet up there by the cairn.'

'Cairn?' enquired Trish.

'A pile of stones,' he replied. 'Understood?'

They nodded and began to walk towards the hill. Nicky and Pip walked together, heads down against the rain. They would have missed the little wooden sign informing them of their location, but Nicky nearly fell over it.

'"Moel Arthur",' Pip read, and they set off to climb the sodden grass mound.

Soon they met up with Jay and Chris, and they climbed together in silence. All they could hear was the pelting rain, the bleating of the ever-present sheep and their own breathing, when, quite suddenly, the rain stopped and the sun came out, dazzling and beautiful. They looked up. They were quite alone. They couldn't see or hear any of the others. 'Where is everyone?' asked Pip nervously.

'They must have gone around the hill – we came straight up from the car park,' explained Chris.

They looked around. It was so quiet up there. The sun shone brightly and the grass felt as though it had springs underneath it. There was a warm breeze blowing through the purple heather and the yellow gorse. The air smelled fresh and pure, and all around them they could see the countryside stretched out like a patchwork quilt of greens, golds and browns.

'The trees down there look like models for a toy railway,' said Chris, breaking the silence.

'It's like being on top of the world,' said Jay.

'It's magic.'

'Look at this!' Nicky's yell of excitement tore the three from the scenery. They looked around, but could not see her.

'What?' asked Jay crossly of the disembodied voice. 'It had better be good…'

'Oh yes, I think you'll find it's good,' said Nicky, her voice full of excitement as she came into view. 'I've found a cave!'

Chapter Ten

'WELL, DID YOU GO IN?' TOM DEMANDED. THEY were in Room Two after lights out. They each had their torches lit and they were sitting in a circle listening intently to Nicky's account of the afternoon's adventure. They hadn't had any time to talk to the others about what had happened without teachers or leaders around to overhear it, so they'd had to wait until nearly ten before they could get together alone. 'It went back and back,' murmured Jay.

'I said, did you go in?' repeated Tom.

'Not all the way,' said Pip.

'Chicken,' growled Tom nastily, and he slouched over to the window and glowered out at the dark.

'It was totally black in there, like completely. As soon as you stood in the entrance the dark sort of grabbed you,' remembered Jay with a shudder.

'You wouldn't have gone in either. Anyway, when I started to walk in, I stood on this.'

On her cue, Nicky opened her hand, and on her palm was a copper-coloured bracelet with a red jewel set in the centre. All the torch-beams were directed towards it, and it glowed in the spotlight. They gasped in amazement. It was beautiful, really beautiful, and it was obviously very old and probably valuable. 'Can I hold it?' asked Andy.

Nicky gave it to him, and he turned it over and over in his hands reverently, inspecting it from every angle.

'I picked it up and dropped it in my pocket,' Jay continued.

'Then we heard footsteps deep inside the cave,' said Nicky, taking over.

'At least two sets, and they were running towards us!' She paused for dramatic effect.

'What did you do?' breathed Sam.

'We legged it,' explained Jay, 'as fast as we could, up to the top where you lot were waiting.'

'But before we ran we looked back and the cave and had gone,' said Nicky. 'There was a mark on the hill where there was no grass, but the cave had disappeared.'

'What have you done?' asked Tom. His voice sounded strange and they all looked up at him, startled.

'What have you done?' he repeated in the same far away voice.

'It's gold all right,' said Andy. 'I'd say you've found something very special, very special.' He handed it back to Nicky.

'It is not yours to keep!' yelled Tom in a booming voice that seemed to fill the building. His face was still turned to the window so they couldn't see his expression, but the voice was terrible enough and they were gripped by dread.

Nicky hastily put the bracelet under her pillow to hide it, exactly why and from whom she didn't really know.

Chris was the first to recover himself, and he went over to Tom, grabbed his arm and slung him round fiercely. 'Shut up you idiot, you'll wake the whole place!'

Then he saw Tom's face. It looked as though it was lit up from inside and his eyes blazed with fury. He appeared taller and older and somehow majestic. Chris let him go and backed away, his eyes round with fear.

Then they heard footsteps and the teachers talking quietly as they walked determinedly towards Room Two.

They leaped into action. Chris and the other boys half dragged, half carried Tom into their room, and Lol and Trish pushed back the bunk. They managed to dive into bed, extinguish the torches and give a pretty convincing performance of innocent slumber as the light snapped on.

Chapter Eleven

B REAKFAST WAS A SUBDUED AFFAIR FOR GROUP One as they eyed Tom nervously.

He hadn't said a thing to anyone since they got up and, if anyone had bothered to look, he still had that strange light behind his eyes.

Fortunately his deep unpopularity with everyone except Joe meant that no one had studied him closely. Joe was talking to him though, but suddenly he stood up angrily and went over to his own group and sat down. Chris made a decision. 'Joe, come over here,' he said.

'What's wrong with him?' asked Joe, nodding in Tom's direction as he walked over to Chris.

'Listen, I'll tell because you're his best friend, but you mustn't breathe a word to anyone else. Promise?'

'Okay, okay, I promise!'

'Swear it!'

'I swear it!' Joe said solemnly. 'What's the big story?'

'Come up to Room Two after breakfast; I'll tell you then.'

'But that's the girls' room!'

'Just be there.'

'Okay.'

Joe sat on Nicky's bunk and listened as they related the events of the previous night. Tom had taken himself off somewhere in the grounds, so they were able to speak freely. Chris had got to the part where the teachers had arrived at Room Two.

'What happened then?' Joe asked,

'Well, the teachers saw that the girls were all asleep – pretty good acting that – and beat a hasty retreat, putting the shouting down to a dream or nightmare,' said Chris.

'Where is it?'

Nicky took the amulet from under her pillow to show him. He gasped, as amazed as they had been when they first saw it. There was no torchlight now, but it still seemed to glow as Nicky held it out for his inspection.

'How could you sleep?' he enquired.

'We were exhausted – you would have been,' said Sam. 'It was all so weird…'

'What did Tom do?'

'We got him into bed and he just lay down and went off into the land of nod as though nothing had happened,' Fred answered.

'But I heard him muttering all sorts of things in his sleep,' said Sam, 'about a lady and lords and stuff.'

'What sort of stuff?' asked Nicky. 'Try to remember.'

'Names mostly; John, Gwyn, Vivienne, *Caledfwlch*…'

'It all makes sense!' Nicky cried.

'I'm glad it makes sense to someone,' muttered Andy, whose down-to-earth and practical nature was rebelling hard in the face of such wonders.

'*Caledfwlch* is the Welsh name for Excalibur, King Arthur's sword.'

'We were on Moel Arthur,' said Pip.

'Hang on,' said Chris and he went to get his map, 'I noticed loads of Arthur places on it yesterday.'

'King Arthur in Wales?' said Andy. 'I thought he lived in Cornwall…'

'Tintagel, he was born there,' said Jay.

'No,' said Joe, 'I happen to know that he was born in Glastonbury because I've been there.'

Fred added, 'There's Arthur's Seat in Edinburgh where he's supposed to be buried with all his knights. I've been there.'

'Look,' said Chris, returning, map in hand. 'I'm right.' He laid the map out on the floor. 'Here at Pen…' He tapped Nicky on the arm.

She looked up from the book she was reading and glanced at the map. 'Penbedw,' she said, and returned to her reading, disappearing into the bunk.

'There's a stone circle where Arthur and his knights are said to be buried.'

'Let's see,' said Sam.

'Look for yourself, it's all here in the bumf on the back.'

Sam looked carefully at the map. 'He seems to have put himself about a bit,' he observed.

'There's where we were yesterday,' said Chris. 'Nannerch. And see? There's another stone circle there.'

They all crowded around the map now – except Nicky, who was still engrossed in her book – and they discovered that they were, indeed, practically surrounded by places where Arthur had either been, or was supposedly buried. There was even a stone at Loggerheads bearing the hoof-prints of his horse. They found Arthur's Well and Arthur's Cauldron at Llangollen. Arthur's Hill at Carven, and Arthur's Vale just down the road from the centre.

'Got it!' announced Nicky appearing from her bunk. She read to them from her book; 'It is possible that the King is buried in Moel Arthur itself, for in a survey dated 1737 there is recorded a cairn or burial chamber with the name Cist Arthur, situated somewhere on the mountain. Tantalisingly, the exact whereabouts of the cist or vault are now unknown. There is a persistent legend in the district that hidden somewhere on Moel Arthur is a treasure. The site of this treasure is said to be illuminated by a pale light shining on the hillside at midnight.' She looked around at the puzzled faces. 'What have we got ourselves mixed up in?'

'Nothing,' said Andy. 'We've not got mixed up in anything at all. You found a cave and picked up a bit of old jewellery, that's all.'

'What about the cave disappearing?' enquired Pip, 'and the running footsteps?'

'An overactive imagination,' said Andy sternly.

'Listen,' said Nicky, 'there's more, about the lake this time...' She read on; '"He spent his last hours in a cave, Ogof y Graig Siagus – the cave of the Shaggy Rocks – after he was mortally wounded in battle. Then he was taken by the Lady of the Lake to Avelon where he sleeps with his knights waiting for the day when Britain will need them in the Final Struggle."'

'The lake was only built in the eighteenth century, remember? You told us that yesterday, Jay,' said Andy.

'The cave could have been there before the lake though, couldn't it?' Jay replied.

'Tell you what,' said Joe, 'we're going there today. I'll dig up what I can about the lake, and we'll visit that cave. Lesley can take some photos and I'll report back tonight.' He stood up and strode purposefully towards the door.

'It won't be there,' said Pip to his retreating back. 'The cave; I bet you it won't be there.'

Chapter Twelve

T HE WEATHER WAS AWFUL, AND A COLD, BITING wind was roaring around the old house. Group One had abseiling on their agenda for the day on a local mountain but, Peter informed them, the weather was too bad for them to abseil in safety, so they were going to a nearby town to use an artificial cliff in the sports centre.

Peter seemed to notice Tom for the first time. He looked at him keenly and said, 'What's the matter lad?'

Tom turned slowly, looked at the group leader with those strange eyes and said, in deep voice that seemed to come from the bowels of the earth, 'There is much the matter, Sir. A dark deed which must be undone.'

'What the...?' Miss Priestly began.

'Oh, it's nothing,' said Trish brightly. 'We've been doing a play together. You know what Nicky's like with her stories,' she added lamely.

The teacher stood up, still looking hard at Tom. 'Get your gear together and we'll go.'

As she left with Peter, Pip heard her say '...keep an eye on that one.'

They managed to cover for Tom's strange behaviour most of the morning, but Miss Priestly and Peter were becoming more and more curious, especially when it was Tom's turn to abseil. His prowess was amazing. He swung up the sheer face with a strength, agility and power that knocked Peter for six. 'Where'd you learn to do that?' he enquired, amazed.

Lest he used that strange voice again, Chris answered, 'Oh, he does it all the time at home, in Royden Park, doesn't he Nicky? With the boy scouts.'

Nicky thought he'd gone too far with the last remark so, as she caught a glint of astonishment in the teacher's eye, she led an animated conversation with the rest of them about Tom's talent and skill, his long and successful membership of the scout movement and their frequent trips to the park to witness his performances.

As they chattered, Miss Priestly turned away. These outdoor pursuit trips certainly gave a teacher a different slant on the children's personalities. She'd had no idea that Tom Harper was so popular, and a boy scout! Then she remembered yesterday, and an image of Tom flailing about in his canoe, stranded in the middle of the lake, came into her mind's eye. It couldn't be the same person, could it?

Tom ignored all that was happening below as he started his descent, continuing to display astonishing skill on the artificial cliff-face. The children applauded his efforts loudly when he reached the ground, surrounding him with a tight wall of admiring fans, before the adults could question him further.

They left the town and Peter drove them back to the centre where, after a tense lunch, they were mercifully sent on an orienteering activity in the grounds, away from the constant scrutiny of adults. They were walking around in the teeth of the continuing gale, when they realised that Tom wasn't with them anymore. They stood for a minute, shouting his name. 'We'd better shut up, or Miss Priestly and Peter will want to know where he is,' said Andy. 'They'll be keeping an eye on us, even though we can't see them.'

'What'd you want?' Tom appeared out of nowhere, looking dishevelled and out of breath.

'You disappeared,' said Jay.

Tom looked around. He seemed back to his old self, but he appeared confused. 'I thought we were going abseiling,' he said. 'What are we doing here?'

Chapter Thirteen

THE OTHERS RETURNED FROM CANOEING AND climbing Moel Arthur, but Joe hadn't anything unusual to report, although Steve had told them that the mountain had once been topped with a hill fort, constructed thousands of years before the birth of Christ and traditionally was said to have been the site of King Arthur's palace.

They were all exhausted, and dinner and the activities in the annex passed in a sort of haze. Tom had stayed with Joe all evening, and had not exchanged a word with his group. He was himself again; moody, difficult, only joining in the games with considerable reluctance. Even Miss Priestly relaxed her surveillance of him after a while, even though, just before dinner, he'd done something so astonishingly out of character, that it had almost left her speechless.

They went to their rooms to write their journals and chat with other groups before lights out, so it wasn't until nearly bedtime that Nicky realised that the bracelet was missing.

She'd checked on it when they got back from orienteering, and it had been safe then, tucked deep under the blue plastic mattress of her bunk. She was bewailing her loss to Trish, Lol and Pip when they heard Joe's voice, raised in anger, coming from Room Seven.

'What did you do that for? I look after you when you get in your moods, smoothing things over and sorting things out, but this time you're on your own!'

They heard the door slam and retreating footsteps, then Mr Gladwell's chastising voice – Joe being on the receiving end presumably – then sobbing, gut-wrenching sobbing coming from the other side of the connecting door.

'Make it stop!' cried Pip. It was a dreadful sound.

Lol leaped to her feet and pushed the bunk away from the door, pulled it open, and there was Tom, sitting on the floor, still crying, with the other boys in a silent, furious circle around him.

'Into bed,' sang Mrs Duffy. 'Lights out in five minutes.'

'Make him shut up,' hissed Lol, 'or we'll all be in trouble.'

They put the room to rights and climbed into bed. They even managed a little small talk with Mrs Duffy when she came in to turn off the light. They listened to the teachers' voices as they sat on the stairs – a nightly ritual they had begun to anticipate – as the chatter in the dorms petered out into silence. As soon as they heard the click of the door of the teachers' lounge closing, they were up and the door into Room Seven was opened. The boys filed silently into the room to tell their story.

Tom, it turned out, had come up to the room, just before dinner, taken the bracelet from Nicky's bunk and given it to Miss Priestly! The girls turned and stared at him in total disbelief. He recoiled from them like a frightened rabbit, and sank to his knees on the floor. Big, tough, Tom Harper, taking something from them and giving it to a teacher! Something so special, so beautiful, so secret!

Tom shrank even more into himself. 'It wasn't yours to keep,' he whispered.

Pip stood up and looked down at him. 'Who told you that?' she asked gently. He looked broken, used, and utterly spent. She felt a sudden wave of pity for him. She went over, stood in front of him and reached down and put her hands on each side of his face, turning it up to her own. 'Tell us what has been happening to you.'

She dropped her hands as he began to talk in a small, faltering voice.

'I don't really know. I felt sort of funny, like there was someone else in my head. Someone powerful, like a warrior. I felt angry, but very afraid. It started when you showed us the bracelet last night,' he said to Nicky.

'I can't quite remember anything about anything after that. I really don't remember going abseiling, honestly.' He looked around at the boys fearfully; there had obviously been some talk on that subject earlier. 'All I knew was that the bracelet had to be placed out of danger, that we mustn't have it in our possession, not in here, not tonight.'

'Why not?' demanded Andy.

'I don't know, but it was – it is – real danger, terrifying, real. I had to protect it, protect you.'

'So you gave it to the teachers?' Lol's voice rose in a crescendo of disbelief.

'I knew I had to give it to a... a...' he faltered, '...a guardian, someone responsible for us. You know how old Gladwell is always going on about being "*in loco parentis*" while we're here, so I gave it to them.' He looked up, some of his usual composure returning, but he still looked drained and exhausted.

'Where is it?' asked Nicky.

'Joe says that they've locked it up in the safe in the office,' said Fred. 'Miss Priestly's going to talk to Peter in the morning. She said something about it being a national treasure, too precious for us to keep.'

'You nerd!' said Sam contemptuously.

'Leave him alone,' ordered Pip. 'Look at the state of him.'

Suddenly a piercing scream tore through the air and the room was suffused in a warm, rosy light. Lol opened the door and peered out into the corridor.

'What's happening?' asked voices, as more children looked out of their rooms. They had to shout above the din, which they now realised was some sort of an alarm.

Someone tried a light switch. The electricity was off and pink emergency lights illuminated the corridors. Lol ventured to the top of the stairs and looked down to see the most incredible sight in the hallway below.

Chapter Fourteen

I T WAS AT 23:47 PRECISELY THAT THE BURGLAR ALARM went off. The teachers were awakened instantly as their dorms were on the ground floor right next to it. They jumped out of bed and Mrs Duffy found the list of instructions that the leaders had left for them should such an emergency arise. She flicked on the light. The electricity was off. The back-up generators kicked in and the emergency lights came on. They picked up the lamps from the office, fumbling about in the pink glow from the corridors, and ran around the building checking for signs of a break-in. Finding that all was secure Mr Gladwell decided that the best thing to do was silence the alarm. He climbed onto a chair to reach the box and followed the instructions that Mrs Duffy read out to him. Miss Priestly continued to check the doors and windows.

Lol and a few other children watched in amazement at the top of the stairs. Mr Gladwell was clad from head to toe in a startlingly white set of long johns, and Mrs Duffy was wearing a long tee-shirt with Sylvester the cat on the back and Tweetie Pie across the front. When Miss Priestly joined them, she had on a white nightie with little cats printed all over it. But what made the scene so surreal was that they were wearing Davey lamp arrangements strapped to their foreheads, so each of them was circled in a dazzling yellow light. Lol relayed this information to the other children in between fits of laughter. 'Miss Priestley's going to make a phone call!' she yelled above the noise. 'Hang on, she's coming back. She's talking to Mrs Duffy. I don't believe it, old Gladwell's taking the batteries out!'

The quiet that followed was bliss. The children ran back into their rooms. There was a loud click as Mr Gladwell changed a fuse, and the strip lights flashed on, and the emergency lights flickered out. The teachers, now demurely attired in their coats and without their halos, walked from room to room to reassure their charges and make sure that no one was upset. Apparently, so they told the children, the alarm was triggered to go off if the electricity failed. It should have stopped after thirty seconds but for some reason, it had gone on ringing so, on Peter's advice, they had taken out the batteries. When they had explained what had happened to everyone and checked that all the children were calm, they turned off the lights and went to bed. After a while, the drama over, everyone settled down to sleep.

Outside there were dark rustlings, but the occupants of the old house slept on unaware.

'Greetings to you, Children of the Dee.'

The deep voice entered the dreams of Group One, and they stirred and opened their eyes. It was still night – deep, dark, inky-black night. At first they couldn't see anything, then the rain clouds rolled away to reveal the moon, round and silver, and they could see the outline of two figures standing by the window.

The boys crept through the dividing door, one by one, and the children stood silent and afraid before the two apparitions. They were like men, but afterwards, when they whispered their recollections to each other, the children couldn't say *what* they really looked like; they had just had a sense of the presence of evil, dark and powerful.

The strange greeting was repeated, the deep voice filling their heads seemingly from within.

The other apparition spoke. 'We are the servants of the Four Horsemen of the Apocalypse. The Wild Beast, rider of the white horse, Victory, who wears the crown of triumph and carries a mighty bow.'

'The rider of the red war-horse, who wields the sword which slays without mercy.'

'The rider of the black horse, Famine, who holds the scales of plenty.'

'The rider of the pale horse, Pestilence, whose name is Death, with all the horrors of Hell in pursuit.' The booming voices stopped.

'What do you want with us?' Tom asked, stepping forward from the rest.

'You know,' the first being replied.

Tom turned to the others. 'They want the bracelet. This is the danger I was warned about.'

'Give it to us!' commanded the voices.

'No,' said Andy, standing next to Tom. 'Why should we?'

'The amulet you stole is King Arthur's. It was set in the entrance to the tomb which holds him, his knights, their squires and chargers too, in enchanted slumber to protect them. You took it from the place called Cist Arthur and now, it is written, we can claim the amulet for our masters. Once it is in their possession, Arthur and all his company will sleep forever, and when the world's end is come, they will not hear the last trumpet. Their souls shall be ever earthbound, ne'er to see the glory of Heaven.'

As these last words were spoken, the children's minds were filled with a terrible despair that was almost too much to bear.

'Why have you told us this?' asked Andy in a whisper.

'You stole the amulet! Tis your transgression broke the spell and now we claim the protector for our masters. It is written in the law.'

Jay stepped forward shaking with dread. 'I took the amulet,' he said.

'Give it to us!'

'No,' he said. 'I can't.'

'Then we shall unleash the powers we have and force your hand,' hissed the first being.

'We know the Gwyllgi, the Dogs of Darkness, and the Cwn Annwn, the Hounds of the Underworld. We walk the paths of evil together, and they will do our bidding.'

'You know what they do?'

The children's heads were filled with visions; snarling, drooling jaws, blazing eyes. Their blood ran cold in their veins and they were terrified. 'Stop!' cried Jay. 'We know what they can do, but we cannot give you the amulet; we have not got it now.'

Again their heads were filled with visions; this time questions, confusion and rage.

That was when Nicky had an idea. She grabbed Lol by the hand and stepped forward. 'We gave it to our Guardians,' she declared. More questions swarmed around their minds. 'Did you not see them at our door?'

Lol suddenly understood. She squeezed Nicky's hand to let her know.

'The one who wears the white suit of purity aided by the shining ones in robes of slumber, protected by the bird and cat!'

'The three who have the light of goodness shining from their brows!' said Nicky triumphantly.

The others, latching on to the theme, continued. 'Did you not hear their cry?'

'It is they that have the amulet now.'

'They guard the door.'

'They are our guardians.'

'They protect us.'

'They are our champions and will keep the amulet from you!'

'We saw the three of whom you speak,' the voices, quieter now, acknowledged. 'We did hear their cry.'

The two figures seemed to shimmer in the moonlight. They were losing their grip on the children's minds, they could feel them pulling away, recognising defeat. Then nothing. They had gone.

Chapter Fifteen

A S THE DAWN BROKE, A MIST HOVERED ABOVE THE lake, a strange grey, swirling fog that twisted and turned as if it was alive.

Tom woke with a start and gazed, stupefied around the scene. How had he got here? He saw the mist, and was aware that the air was full of whisperings. He crouched down behind a canoe and watched and listened, every nerve in his body zinging.

'The amulet is taken, Lady.' The words rose from the mist like a whisper.

'I know it,' came the reply.

The grey mist was turning slowly in a spiral like a gentle tornado. It was joined by another, pure white, shivering in the watery morning sunshine. Suddenly the two swirls spun, whipping across the still water, and stopped on the grassy shore. There stood two women – so close to Tom that he could have reached out and touched them – one grey, one white, in long, billowing robes, their veiled faces drooped to the earth with sorrow.

The grey lady spoke again. 'I only guard the treasure after midnight, when the pale light bathes the door.'

'Yours is not the blame, sister,' replied the white lady, and she took the other by the hand.

'You know, then, who tis that caused this harm?' she asked.

The white lady nodded. 'Two squires, the ones whom for this last century have been the guards. It is they who opened the door, for only I with Caledfwlch Excalibur can smite the rock and open the door from outside. No, they must have opened it from within.'

'But tis forbidden!' gasped the grey lady.

'They did not heed,' the white lady sighed. She lifted her head. 'Who goes there?'

Tom watched, amazed, as two boys about his age appeared out of the mist. They were dressed in tabards like the medieval squires he'd seen at Camelot Theme Park when he was little. They both knelt before the women, their heads hung in shame.

'John,' said the first boy, 'squire to Sir Bors, strongest of Arthur's Knights, cousin of Sir Lancelot, brave and true, and a knight who sought the grail, Lady.'

The second boy spoke; 'Gwyn, squire of Sir Percival, the one called Fool, who became wise and saw the blessed grail with pure Sir Galahad, son of Sir Lancelot.'

'I know the knights you serve,' said the white lady sternly. 'They slumber still?'

'Aye, Lady,' replied John.

'Forever, and without their soul's release, methinks, John, squire of Sir Bors.'

'But Lady…'

'Peace boy,' she said more kindly, and touched him lightly on his hair.

She turned to the other. 'Gwyn, whose name means white, who serves wise Sir Percival, what say you?'

'We opened the door, Lady.'

'It is forbidden!' she rasped. Her anger was terrible to see.

'We opened the door,' Gwyn repeated flatly, as though all the hope in the world had died.

'Why?' interrupted the grey lady, her voice full of questions.

'To see the sun,' said John.

'To feel the wind,' Gwyn added.

'Hear them sister, the sun, the wind!' snarled the white lady.

'The sun and wind your lords and Arthur will never now see,' said the grey lady sadly.

'What can we do?' asked John.

'Who took the amulet?' demanded the white lady.

'Four children came to the entrance, it was they who took the amulet. We ran, but the door, enchanted, shut,' said Gwyn.

'We beg forgiveness!' cried John desperately.

'That you shall not have until the amulet is returned,' said the white lady in reply to his pleading. 'And you can do nought but wait.'

'We have waited and watched for o'er a hundred years, Lady. We were tired of the darkness of the cave,' John wailed.

'The new watch did not come, even though the

century waned and a new one began,' said Gwyn. He stifled a sob. 'The new watch did not come.'

The white lady ignored his weeping and turned to John. 'Tired, were you boy? You *will* be tired for this transgression! I may condemn you to another hundred years on guard if this sorry deed is not put to rights. Now go and do your duty.'

The boys stumbled to their feet, walked away, and were lost once more in the mist of the lake.

Tom breathed deeply, silently. Maybe he'd wake up and find this was all a dream... but he could feel the wet grass and the rough side of the canoe; he was really here.

'I saw the children of whom they speak,' said the white lady. 'They came first to the lake where I must guard Excalibur in the cave of the Shaggy Rocks. Come, sister, I see a hope here. We must visit these children and ensure the safe return of the amulet.'

'If I look on mortals, they will die,' warned the grey lady.

'No harm must come to them, or all is lost,' retorted the white lady, alarmed.

'I will hide my eyes from them. This my promise be.'

'I thank you,' said the white lady. 'Now I must intone spells into the Cursing Well at Llanelwan-y-Rhos to thwart the Four Horsemen, and from thence go to the holy well at Llangollen, called Arthur's Well, to call upon the Fisher King. For it is he, King Pelleam – whose wound was healed by the Grail Knights and whose kingdom, Listinios, the Waste Land, was made whole – who guards the true Grail and has power over spirits in this place older than King Arthur, before our time, sister.'

'The wells may now be lost, Lady.'

'Not lost, only covered o'er. The power remains. I will away, sister, and beseech the Fisher King to aid these mortals who, all unknowing, have placed our King in such danger.' She turned to the water of the lake, lifted her hands in supplication and spoke a prayer.

'The starry King will watch and wait;
The Guardian of the Golden Gate,
The keeper of the Seven Seals,
The eyes of fire, the hand that heals –
At your feet this lady kneels.

These mortals took the charm that tried
The secret of the cavern to hide.
Protect us from the Four from Hell.
And break the curse, restore the spell.
Take them where the sleepers dwell.

The sunset sky will light the way,
The Dogs of Darkness run and bay.
The Hounds of Hell unleashed will be,
The dragon rides the stormy sea.
Come, in my torment pity me.

Mere mortals they have stumbled in,
Committing an unknowing sin.
Please, in your goodness lead them on,
So they can right this dreadful wrong,
To Arthur's cave where it belong.'

Without warning, the women turned once more into whirling pillars of mist and spun across the lake. Tom's ears were filled with a roaring so loud he was forced to cover them to block out the sound, but the roaring went on and on until he slid to the ground unconscious.

Chapter Sixteen

A T BREAKFAST THE NEXT DAY ALL THE CHILDREN in Group One looked so awful that the leaders and teachers went together to the annex to hold a special meeting.

Tom hadn't woken up that morning and the boys had had to tell the adults about his condition. They had gathered around his bed, talking in whispers. They were going to call a doctor and wait until he had been examined and then, if necessary, call his parents to come and pick him up. Mr Gladwell had lifted Tom out of his bunk as if he weighed nothing more than a feather and carried him gently down to the sick room on the ground floor with a tenderness the children marvelled at.

Peter returned from the meeting to the canteen and addressed the anxious children. 'Now, there's nothing for you to look so worried about. The doctor's with Tom now and she says he's suffering from nothing worse than exposure.'

'Exposure?' exploded Joe. 'How's...?'

Peter silenced him with a look. 'As I was saying, Tom's going to be fine. There's no need for phone calls to school or home – he'll be fine, a day in bed in the warm...' He trailed off and sat down at the teachers' table, still littered with breakfast things, clearly rattled by the turn of events. The other adults had returned and Miss Priestly took over. 'We'll continue with our programme as planned.'

There were some quiet cheers at this news.

'Groups Two, Three and Four can go to their meeting rooms at once and get ready for today's agenda,' barked Mr Gladwell, back to his old self again. 'Come on, chop, chop!'

With that, he marched out towards the annex with the chattering children following behind, clearly relieved that things were back to normal.

Joe shot Chris a look as he left, who shrugged and mouthed, 'See you later,' to him.

The exchange was noted by Miss Priestly, and she and Peter surveyed Group One with dark eyes. 'As for you lot,' she said, 'you're staying right here. You've got some explaining to do.' She sat down next to Peter and held out her hand. She was holding the amulet. 'Tell me all about this.'

'Everything, chapter and verse,' added Peter gravely. 'Now!'

Chapter Seventeen

I T WAS MOST RELUCTANTLY THAT PETER AND MISS Priestly let the children go back to their rooms to think things over.

They met in Room Two and sat on the bunks, silent and troubled. 'We couldn't tell them, could we?' asked Pip.

'No,' said Chris. 'They wouldn't believe it. I don't think I believe it either.'

'But what happened to Tom?' asked Trish. 'How did he get exposure in bed?'

Andy got to his feet wearily. 'Someone's got to get to him and find out,' he announced.

'Miss Priestly's sitting with him and Peter's in the teachers' lounge right next door. They won't let us see him. They don't believe all that stuff about a midnight feast, Fred, even coming from you,' said Lol.

'It was the best I could come up with,' he growled.

'But we've got to see him,' said Andy.

'Why?' asked Nicky. 'What do you think he knows?'

'Oh, come on, storyteller, surely you can see there's something weird going on here? And it's all connected to that amulet you stole, Jay.'

'I didn't steal it,' said Jay petulantly.

'Those guys who came here last night certainly thought you did,' said Sam.

'I've got an idea,' said Andy. 'Listen...'

As soon as Nicky knocked on the teachers' lounge door, Peter opened it.

'Can I talk to you?' she asked.

'Come in,' said Peter. 'The truth this time. Close the door.'

At the same time Lol knocked quietly on the sick room door. When Miss Priestly opened it she burst into tears and flung herself at the teacher. 'I want to go home!' she wailed, 'I want to go home! I want to phone my mum, but I can't, I've lost my purse!'

'Shh, shh,' comforted Miss Priestly, 'we mustn't wake Tom. Come through here and tell me all about it.' And she led the sobbing child into the canteen, closing the door softly behind her.

As soon as she heard the door of the canteen shut, Pip slid silently into the sick room. Tom would surely talk to her.

Andy stood in the shadows at the top of the stairs, watching. He turned and gave the thumbs up to the others in Room Two. All they had to do now was wait.

When the girls returned they each related their part of the plan, and then it was Pip's turn.

'He looks terrible,' she said, 'but he did talk a little.' She paused and took a deep breath. 'He says we've done something really bad, and there're people – beings, ghosts – that want the amulet back.'

'We know, we've met them,' said Chris.

'No, not just them, other people he saw this morning by the lake.'

'But…' began Andy.

'Let her speak,' commanded Chris. 'There's no sense to this, as I think we all realise, so we'll just have to go with the flow.'

'He says they want to see us and that we've got to go down to the lake as soon as possible. We've got to give the amulet back tonight. He said he trusts these ghosts and that they will help us.'

'I'm sure Peter will let some of us go out. He really bought the story about us being worried about the police because we think we've done something wicked,' said Nicky.

'It's got to be you four,' said Lol. 'You went into the cave.'

'Okay, okay,' said Fred, 'but how are we going to get the amulet out of the safe?'

'You keep Peter happy and I can open that safe, no problem,' said Andy.

'You can?' said Pip. 'Really?'

'Yes, I've seen where they keep the key.'

'Miss Priestly won't leave Tom's side. She was kind to me when I was crying to go home, but she was much more worried about Tom,' said Lol.

'You go and see Peter, leave the rest to us.'

And so it was decided, and the children went out, each to their appointed task.

Chapter Eighteen

I T WAS A LOVELY AFTERNOON. THE SKY WAS BLUE and the birds were singing. The four of them were lying on the grass by the lake. The centre and all their troubles inside seemed a long way away.

'Are you sure he meant this lake?' asked Jay.

'Well, it's the only lake we can get to. I can't see Peter letting us drive the minibus to Ysgeifiog,' said Nicky.

They lay on the grass in silence for a moment.

'Do you believe all this King Arthur stuff?' Jay asked.

'I went to a place called "Knights' Caverns" once in Rhyl. That was all about King Arthur. It was really good. It had all that stuff about the Dogs of Darkness and evil goblins,' said Chris.

'And I've been to another one when I went to my auntie's. It's in Corris in a slate mine, right inside the mountain. You go in and a boat comes to get you, then you sail along and get out at a landing stage. It's really dark and freezing cold. Then a monk comes along and guides you through tunnels into huge caverns, and there're life-size models of Merlin, King Arthur and his knights. They light up and voices tell you the stories. It's brilliant.' Nicky lay back and smiled, remembering.

'So it could be true...' whispered Pip.

Jay sat up. 'Listen,' he said. They all strained to hear.

'Nothing,' said Chris.

'Exactly.'

They knew what Jay meant; there wasn't a sound. The birds had stopped singing, the breeze was still.

'Look!' said Pip in amazement, pointing to the lake. 'Look!'

There, out of the silent water, a hand and then an arm appeared, a veiled head, then a body, draped in the purest white. Up and up the figure rose without a sound or a ripple. Then, without warning, she was standing next to them, smiling sadly. 'You are the children of the Dee?' she asked, her voice a sweet whisper inside their heads.

'We have been greeted as such before,' said Nicky, rising to her feet.

The others did the same and stood before the lady, feeling awed and afraid.

'I am the Lady of the Lake. I am Nynyne, who took my lord, King Arthur, to Avelon. I am Nimue who captured the heart of Merlin the wizard and imprisoned him beneath a stone. I am Niniane who gave Excalibur to Arthur, but you may know me as the Lady Vivienne who guards Excalibur still.' Her voice was soft and low and they were all entranced. Suddenly the tone changed. 'You have placed my lord and all his entourage in great danger!'

'We know,' said Jay.

'How know you?' she asked.

'Two servants of the Four Horsemen of the Apocalypse came last night to claim the amulet we found in the cave on Moel Arthur for their masters,' he replied.

'They have it?' she asked in terror.

'No,' said Nicky.

'How stayed you the wrath of Hell?' she breathed, amazed.

'We gave the amulet to our teachers. They had it in safe keeping.'

'Tis providential that you have such powerful guardians to protect you,' she said. 'Who took the amulet? Speak!' she commanded.

'I did,' said Jay.

'Then you must get it from your guardians and place the amulet back in Cist Arthur tonight at midnight when the pale light shines.'

'But he can't,' declared Nicky. 'It's too dangerous.'

'You know of the Grey Lady who guards the treasure that can turn a mortal to stone with one look?'

Nicky nodded.

'Fear not. She met me at the lake at dawn today. She knows what is to be and will turn her eyes from you. She promised then.'

'Will she keep her promise?'

'Yes.'

'What must we do then?' asked Jay.

'A noble king who owes King Arthur and his Grail Knights a great favour has agreed to deliver you from the Gwyllgi and the Cwn Annwn along the path of evil. The Golden Spectre of Goblin Hill will carry you along the way, the Fisher King has awakened him and he will do his bidding.'

'I've read about him!' declared Nicky.

'Then you will know him?'

'Oh yes,' she said. 'He is a shining, golden giant who wears a great gold collar over ancient armour and a necklace of many amber beads.'

'Your teachers must indeed be wise to impart this ancient knowledge to their apprentices. You will know him then. He will come from his Goblin Mountain at Pentre tonight to your dwelling here, just before midnight. Have the amulet from your guardians and keep it with you. Be sure in this and have steady hearts, children of the Dee, for by your hand is this danger come, and by your hands only can this be undone.' Then their heads were filled with music, soft and soothing, and the lady sang to them.

'Kings and princes, knights and knaves,
Do wander where the Hell Hound bays.
Dragons lie in hills and caves
Along the paths of evil ways.

'Lighted by the silver moon,
Is the warrior in his tomb.
On the lanes of darkening gloom
The curs lure travellers to their doom.

'Where the warring swordsmen fled
And found the cave to lay their dead.
"Be not afraid," the lady said,
"Though filled with wonder, awe and dread."

'You have stumbled on the home
Of goblin, spectre and of gnome.
Mists of time have softly blown,
And you must wander out alone.

'On our aid you can depend,
King and knights we must defend.
Help and guidance we will send
To take you to your journey's end.'

A light breeze lifted their hair and when they looked up she was gone.

Chapter Nineteen

T HE OTHER GROUPS CAME BACK FULL OF HAPPY chatter about gorge-walking, canoeing and abseiling. Mr Gladwell questioned Peter and Miss Priestly closely about the day at the centre, and was relieved to see that Group One were in the clear and that everyone seemed to be in good spirits. Even Tom was out of bed and was coming to dinner with the rest.

It was the night when the catering staff gave up their kitchen to the visitors, and the children were to prepare and serve their own meal. And so the evening was taken up with everyday activities such as designing menus, peeling vegetables and fruit and, of course, cooking. No one would ever forget the saga of Miss Duffy's group and the custard, but that's another story...

It was great. The meal, though unusual, was declared a huge success, and by the time they'd cleared up it was well past bedtime. The children were asleep almost before their heads touched their pillows. Tom, the teachers had insisted, was to sleep in the sick room that night. Pip managed to tell him that they had met the Lady of the Lake and that the amulet would be returned to the hill at midnight. He was still so exhausted that all he could manage was a weak, 'Thank you,' before he went meekly, ushered off to bed by Miss Priestly.

And so it was that the teachers' stint on the stairs was a short-lived affair that night and, after the pressures of the day, they too went straight to bed.

They were all there in Room Two, torches on, and Andy had the amulet for Jay to take.

'We're coming with you,' said Chris. 'Nicky, Pip, get ready.'

They dressed in outdoor clothes and Jay borrowed the schoolbag Fred had brought his special emergency rations in to hold the amulet. It was neater and smaller than the rucksacks provided by the centre. Jay felt that it would be wrong to drag the amulet out of his pocket, when the time arrived, so he wrapped it carefully in one of the big white handkerchiefs his mother had insisted on him bringing on the trip, and placed it gently inside the bag. They were ready. It was almost midnight.

They heard the voice again, Lady Vivienne singing inside their heads, in the room, the house, the countryside – the sound was everywhere, filling the night with music.

'Children of the River Dee,
Dwellers by the waning sea.
Come to me,
Come to me,
Come to my water,
My son and my daughter,
Come to me.

'Children of the wilderness,
Walkers by the choking grass.
Come to me,
Come to me,
One way or the other,
My sister, my brother.
Come to me.

'Children of the Wirral, yet
Takers of the amulet.
Come to me,
Come to me,
My King he entreats thee,
You must come to meet me.
Come to me.'

As the song finished they saw that the room was flooded with a golden light. A huge gauntleted hand was outside the window, turning slowly until it came to a rest with palm outstretched.

'The Golden Spectre!' said Andy. 'I don't believe it.'

Fred and Sam opened the window as wide as it would go, and the hand came closer until it touched the sill.

'Go on,' urged Lol.

'Good luck,' whispered Trish.

The four children climbed up into the casement and walked unsteadily onto the mailed glove. The golden light blotted out everything, but they could hear the creaking of great leather boots, the clunk of heavy armour and the tapping of many beads.

The hand closed around them, shutting out the light, and they crouched in the darkness, filled with abject terror, in their strange transport. Suddenly there was a mighty thunderclap and the sound of many horses ridden at full gallop. The giant roared and the children covered their ears against the inhuman cry. They were aware of movement, running, thunderous footsteps pounding down the lanes. Great hounds bayed at their heels and the beat of hooves crashed behind them.

Chapter Twenty

LADY VIVIENNE HEARD THE THUNDER TOO. SHE came to Cist Arthur with Caledfwlch Excalibur. 'Is it time?' she asked.

A pale light hovered at shoulder height. As Tom looked up, he could see it. 'Not again,' he moaned. He was too tired to even try to hide, and so he lay on the grass where he had found himself, watching and listening.

'Almost, Lady,' came the reply. 'He has carried the mortals here and laid them down atop.'

As she spoke, the Grey Lady shimmered into view. She wore a dark veil to cover her eyes, keeping her promise. Tom looked up, and there above him, sprawled on the summit, were Chris, Nicky, Pip and Jay.

A huge roar rocked the ground and they could hear the sound of hoof-beats and the baying of great hounds.

'The mortals! I do fear for them!' cried Lady Vivienne. 'The Four Horsemen are come!'

'Look,' said the Grey Lady, 'the giant leads them away. They must follow him.'

Huge rumblings filled the air as the gleaming giant strode away across the hills. The golden light grew dimmer as he went. The hooves of the terrible horses thundered all around them, unseen. 'Where are the mortals?' a voice roared.

'Follow them yonder, quickly, go!' cried the Grey Lady, pointing to the receding light. 'They have the Golden Spectre in their thrall and go now to his Goblin Hill.'

'Who dared awake the giant from his enchanted slumber?' a voice boomed.

'The Fisher King!' Lady Vivienne cried in triumph.

The night was filled with a roar of anguish more terrible than the listeners had ever heard, or would ever wish to hear again.

When it was over, the voices spoke again. 'The Fisher King knows of this?'

'He knows.'

'He rides from Listinios?'

'He rides this night.'

'It cannot be! Now is not the time for the final battle, the last trumpet does not sound! We cannot ride the earth together until that time is come. We must away!'

The hoof-beats began again, thundering, crashing, roaring through the air and the Hell Hounds bayed. Then came a smell; fetid, evil, burning, acid fumes that made eyes run with tears and stomachs heave.

Slowly, slowly the noise receded and the stench began to clear.

'Now!' whispered the Grey Lady.

Lady Vivienne raised the sword above her head in both hands and brought it down with tremendous force on the grey stone that marked the cave. The earth rumbled and Tom watched as a dark entrance appeared in the side of the hill. The children scrambled down from above, and Jay walked forward, the other three behind him, and took the amulet carefully from the bag, unwrapped it and placed it on the ground in the doorway to the cave.

It lay, glowing with its eerie light.

Two dark figures slithered onto the scene. Tom recognised them at once.

'We come to claim the amulet for our masters, the Four...'

'Enough!' cried Lady Vivienne. 'I know the masters whom you serve. They have returned to the underworld and will not come again till Judgement Day is nigh.'

'Then we claim the amulet for ourselves!'

The black figures slid forwards in a rapid, sinuous, flowing movement towards the cave.

'Hold!' cried the Grey Lady.

'They are of the world's end, you cannot do them harm,' Lady Vivienne warned.

'But I can stay them with my gaze! Hold, I say. Give me your eyes!' and she threw back her veil.

'Look away!' Lady Vivienne commanded the children.

The figures stopped and turned towards the Grey Lady, unwilling but bound so to do, and they met her gaze and froze like statues, fastened to the spot.

Tom looked back towards the cave and saw a light far inside the hill. It was getting nearer and nearer and soon he could make out the two boys he had seen by the lake. They each carried a flaming torch, held up high. They stopped by the entrance and knelt down before Lady Vivienne.

'For the king, great Arthur, our lords, Sir Bors, Sir Percival and all our company, we thank you,' said the one called John.

'It is these mortal children you should thank.' She drew all the children to her. 'And you, Tom,' she said. He stood up, amazed, and joined the group. 'They have returned the amulet, which you so recklessly revealed, at great peril to their lives and to their souls.' The boys dropped their eyes and mumbled thanks.

'Go now and sleep, and I shall appoint another two to guard this century around. You are reprieved.'

The boys stood up, bowed gravely to them all, turned and were lost in the shadows of the cave.

'Lady! I cannot hold them any longer!' the Grey Lady cried, awakening them to the danger which had not passed.

'The dawn is here,' Lady Vivienne sighed and smiled. 'Release them, they belong to the dark and cannot tarry now. It is we who have done this good deed who have a place in the sun.'

The Grey Lady dropped her gaze and hid her eyes once more behind her veil and the two figures simply melted into the earth.

Lady Vivienne touched the entrance to the cave with the sword and the rock face sealed the way, then she turned and smiled at each child in turn. 'You have done well. Whatever enchantment I must do, you will each remain bound in friendship because of your work this night.' She looked at Tom and lifted his face, her hand cupped around his chin. 'You of all were chosen by Arthur to lead the way. You have an old soul and a good heart. Live long and be happy.' And then the air was filled with music, beautiful and enchanted. Lady Vivienne began to sing.

'Children of the River Dee,
Dwellers by the waning sea.
O'er your heads enchantment flows
All memory of your adventure goes...

'Sister, I will take them home and chant this spell o'er all the house. Farewell.'

Chapter Twenty-one

THE CHILDREN IN GROUP ONE WOKE UP IN THEIR bunks, refreshed and happy. Then they remembered; Tom was still in the sick room.

A tap came on the adjoining door and Chris's face peered round. 'Not up yet?' he asked. 'Hurry up, we're going to see Tom.'

They listened to the boys clatter down the stairs and then got out of bed and pulled on their clothes; washing could wait. They opened the door and the boys were standing on the landing. Tom was there.

'Clean bill of health,' he said. 'They reckon I got a chill or something when we went canoeing. Miss Priestly's set me free!'

They hurtled into breakfast, looking forward to the day ahead.

'What are we doing today?' asked Pip.

'Gorge-walking,' said Tom.

'Brilliant!' she exclaimed, and she and Tom sat down together, talking and laughing happily as they tucked into a hearty breakfast.

Miss Priestly looked aghast. Mrs Duffy sat with her spoon laden with cornflakes suspended halfway between the bowl and her mouth.

'See,' said Mr Gladwell, rubbing his hands

together, 'I told you it would be the making of her.'

'Of her?' said Mrs Duffy, and she smiled at Miss Priestly. 'If you'd have told me yesterday... amazing.'

'A miracle,' Miss Priestly agreed.

Oh, and the name Group One finally gave their headquarters was 'Goblin Hill', though no one knew why.

Further Reading

Coghlan, Ronan, *The Illustrated Encyclopaedia of Arthurian Legends*, (Element Books Limited, 1993)

Gantz, Jeffrey (translator), *The Mabinogion*, (Penguin Books Ltd., 1976)

Holland, Richard, *Supernatural Clwyd*, (Gwasg Carreg Gwalch, 1989)

Knights' Caverns – The Guidebook (H B Leisure)

Lister, Robin, *The Story of King Arthur*, (Kingfisher Books, 1994)

Matthews, John & Bob Stewart, *Legends of King Arthur and his Warriors*, (Blandford Press, 1987)

Matthews, John, *The Arthurian Tradition*, (Element Books Limited, 1989)

Snowdonia & North Wales Ordnance Survey Touring Map & Guide 10

Pronunciation

With thanks to Terry Duffy

Moel Famau	'Moil Vammer'
Gwyllgi	'(G)wiskee'
Clwyd	'Cloyid'
Cwn Annwn	'Keen Anwen'
Ysgeifiog	'Asskiveiog'
Ogof y Graig Siagus	'Ogoth a Grige Shaggis'
Penbedw	'Penbedoo'
Caledfwlch	'Caledvulch' (guttural)
Nannerch	'Nanerch' (guttural)
Llanelwan-y-Rhos	'Thlanelwan a Chorse'
Eglwysed	'Eglooisaid'
Llangynhafal	'Chlginhavil'